WATERSHIP DOWN

We Need
More Rabbits!

Jason Hamish Millar

Tel...01463/793472

Other
Watership Down
fiction adventures

We Need More Rabbits!

Judy Allen

RED FOX

A Red Fox Book

Published by Random House Children's Books
20 Vauxhall Bridge Road, London SW1V 2SA

A division of The Random House Group Ltd
London Melbourne Sydney Auckland
Johannesburg and agencies throughout the world

Text and illustrations © 1999 Alltime Entertainment Ltd.
and DECODE Entertainment Inc.

www.watershipdown.net

Illustrations by County Studio, Leicester

1 3 5 7 9 10 8 6 4 2

Printed and bound in Denmark by Nørhaven A/S

THE RANDOM HOUSE GROUP Limited Reg. No. 954009

www.randomhouse.co.uk

ISBN 0 09 940375 7

This story represents scenes from
the television series, Watership Down,
which is inspired by Richard Adams'
novel of the same name.

Contents

❧───────❧

The Characters of Watership Down

Hazel

The leader of the group, Hazel persuaded
his friends to leave their old warren at
Sandleford and start a new life elsewhere.

Fiver

One of the youngest rabbits, Hazel's brother
Fiver has visions of the future – a gift that
sometimes causes him many problems.

Bigwig

A former member of the Sandleford Owsla,
Bigwig naturally uses force to settle any
disputes and has no time for time-wasters.

Pipkin

The youngest and most vulnerable rabbit,
Pipkin is innocent, sweet and adventurous,
and a well-loved friend to all the group.

Blackberry

An intelligent doe, Blackberry is a great problem solver and at times of crisis, she is the calm voice of reason.

Hawkbit

Hawkbit is always ready to look on the glum side, but when the going gets tough, his loyalty to the group shines through.

Dandelion

Talker, joker and storyteller, Dandelion is always ready to celebrate the heroic deeds of the warren and El-Arah.

Kehaar

A newcomer to the group, Kehaar thinks he's much cleverer than the rabbits, but infact he can't manage without them.

Hannah

A fearless fieldmouse, Hannah often tends to forget her size and has no problem trading insults with bigger animals.

BEANFIELD

NUTHANGER FARM

WATE
DO

PEAT BOG

THE HEATHER

COWSLIP'S
WARREN

ENBORNE RIVER
CROSSING

THE WORLD OF

WATERSHIP
DOWN

N

LAD
HIL

STATELY MANSION

UPPER
BRIDGE

EFRAFA

LOWER
BRIDGE

RAILWAY
ARCH

RAILWAY CROSSING

WHITCHURCH

CHAPTER ONE

An Empty Warren

The warren was finished at last. Its burrows ran deep under the roots of a beech tree, on the crest of Watership Down. All the rabbits were inside, admiring their new home.

'Good and strong,' said Bigwig. 'The rain won't get in here.'

'And there's plenty of space,' said Blackberry, proudly. She had planned the network of burrows and done most of the digging herself.

Hazel was the only one who didn't look happy.

'What's bothering you?' said Bigwig.

Hazel looked around at his group –
his younger brother Fiver, Bigwig and
Blackberry, Hawkbit and Dandelion,
Strawberry and little Pipkin.

'There are so few of us,' said Hazel.
'We'll be lost in here.'

He hopped outside, and when Bigwig and Fiver followed they found him watching the sky.

'I'm waiting for Kehaar,' he said.

'That gull's always sky-wandering,' said Fiver. 'He could be anywhere.'

'I asked him to fly to the Efrafa warren,' said Hazel, 'and report back.'

'Whatever for?' said Bigwig.

'We need more rabbits,' said
Hazel simply.

'But Hazel,' said Fiver, 'the
Efrafans are vicious and aggressive!'

'And from what I hear of General
Woundwort, their leader,' said
Bigwig, 'he'd tear you to bits
on sight!'

'Exactly,' said Hazel.
'There must be rabbits
there who'd be glad
to leave.'

'Ah,' said Bigwig.
'Good thinking.'
And he and Fiver
began to watch
the sky, too.

When Kehaar returned from
Efrafa, he brought news of a grim,
dark warren ruled by fear.

The Watership Down rabbits
listened in horror as he described
what he had seen. He told them
about a buck called Blackavar
who'd tried to escape, but was

hunted down and dragged before Woundwort himself. He told them about the terrible moment when Woundwort sentenced Blackavar to death. He told how a brave doe called Primrose pleaded for Blackavar's life, and how Woundwort had threatened her with the same punishment.

And that, said Kehaar, was when he took action. 'Kehaar go for rotten bully Woundwort!' he squawked, and he launched himself into the air to show how he had flown at the Efrafan rabbits. 'Kehaar made 'em run!' he shrieked. 'Then fly back here.'

'Imagine living like that!' said Fiver, when the gull had finished his story.

'If Woundwort finds Watership Down before we're up to strength,' said Bigwig, 'You won't have to imagine it.'

Hazel nodded. 'That settles it,' he said. 'We must go to Efrafa before Efrafa comes to us.'

CHAPTER TWO

Danger in Efrafa

The journey to Efrafa was long and sometimes frightening. Hazel took Bigwig and Fiver with him, and Kehaar flew above to show the way.

They hopped and rested, rested and hopped, until the sun set and a bright moon rose.

Kehaar led them to the long ridge of a railway embankment and up the side. At the top they stared in surprise at the steel rails, shining silver in the moonlight.

'What's this?' said Fiver.

'Looks like a giant double slug-trail,' said Bigwig.

'I wouldn't want to meet the slug that left it!' said Hazel.

They began to cross, but before
they were half way a strange
rumbling sound shook the rails.

'They're alive!' said Bigwig.

The rumbling grew closer, lights
blazed and something enormous
came roaring towards them.

'Run!' shouted Hazel, and they
bolted just in time. The train missed
them by inches as it clattered past.

'What was that thing?' panted Bigwig, but none of them knew.

'This way,' came a shriek from the sky, and on they travelled, while the night faded and the sun rose once more.

'Are we nearly there, Kehaar?' said Fiver.

'Not far now,' the gull squawked back.

And then, right in the middle of a field, the shadow of a tall man fell across them.

'Scatter!' shouted Bigwig.

The rabbits dived for cover, but Kehaar

laughed and landed on the man's
hat.

Hazel approached the figure
cautiously. 'It's not real,' he said.
'It's stuffed with straw,' said Fiver.
'It's enough to scare a
crow,' said Bigwig,
crossly.

'It got you jumping,' said Kehaar.

Bigwig frowned and changed the subject. 'So where's Efrafa?' he said.

'You go careful,' said Kehaar. 'We very near.' He landed and waddled towards a hedge of brambles. They peered through the thorns and saw a gloomy warren dug into a bank, under the twisted branches of a dead tree.

Nearby, the Efrafans were nibbling grass, in orderly lines, watched over by fierce-looking guards.

'Rabbits weren't meant to live like that,' said Fiver, shocked.

Kehaar pointed with a wing. 'Over there,' he said. 'That Blackavar. And that Primrose.'

'Primrose,' said Hazel dreamily. He crept forwards, hidden by brambles, until he was close enough for her to hear him. 'Primrose,' he whispered, 'I'm Hazel – we've come to get you out of here.'

'Be careful,' Primrose whispered back. 'Woundwort spared us because

I pretended Blackavar was running from a gull, not trying to escape. Now those two Owsla captains – Campion and Vervain – are watching us.'

At that moment, Fiver stepped on a twig, which cracked loudly. Vervain rose on his haunches and stared towards Hazel's hiding place.

'Run, Blackavar!' said Primrose, and the two rabbits bolted. Instantly Vervain and Campion took off after them. They were caught in seconds.

'She saved us!' said Hazel.

'She plenty brave bunny,' said Kehaar.

'We have to rescue her,' said Hazel fiercely. 'Blackavar, too.'

'How?' said Bigwig.

Fiver crouched low,
eyes closed and ears
twitching, as one of
his visions filled his
mind. 'The only
way out is to go
straight through,'
he said. 'If two go in,
then out come two.'

'Right,' said Hazel.
'Two will go in. Bigwig, stay here
with Kehaar. If it all goes wrong, you
must take over at Watership Down.'
He turned to Fiver. 'Ready, little
brother?'

Fiver nodded.

'You're mad,' said Bigwig. 'But
good luck anyway.'

The two Owsla captains had marched Primrose and Blackavar to the warren entrance and were about to take them inside. Vervain had a weasel-like face but Campion looked dignified and honest, so Hazel hopped up to him. 'Take me to your leader,' he said, calmly.

Before Campion could speak, Vervain began to shout orders. 'All rabbits to the gathering place. Let everyone watch the General deal with these intruders.'

Slowly the Efrafans, Primrose and Blackavar

among them, formed a half-circle in
front of the warren. Every rabbit
looked up at a platform, held by
the claw-like roots of the
dead tree above.

Vervain pushed Hazel and Fiver forwards, and General Woundwort stepped out of the shadows – a huge, grey rabbit, cold-eyed and battle-scarred.

'You demand to see me?' he said, glowering down at them. 'Well I have no interest in stray rabbits!' He signalled to the Owsla captains. 'Execute them on my command!' he snarled.

Vervain and Campion moved closer, foreclaws raised, ready to strike.

Woundwort leant forwards, his glittering eyes fixed on Hazel. 'Where is your warren?' he snarled. 'Tell me, and live.'

'I can't do that, General,' said
Hazel.

Woundwort straightened up. 'Kill
them!' he roared. 'Kill them both.'

CHAPTER THREE

A Shock for Woundwort

Just as the Owsla captains were about to strike, Fiver let out a strange, eerie cry. The captains stopped, taken by surprise. 'Oh,' Fiver wailed, rocking to and fro, eyes closed. 'Oh. Stormhaven is destroyed!'

High on his platform, Woundwort
drew in his breath with a hiss.
'Wait!' he snapped.

Campion and Vervain stepped
back in confusion.

'The field is on fire,' Fiver moaned, 'The warren is burning – Laurel – save him –'

His words had an extraordinary effect.

'Laurel,' said Woundwort, in a soft voice no one had heard before. 'Laurel. My mother.' Then he shouted, 'Clear the gathering place! Everyone underground.'

The Efrafans filed obediently into the warren. As Primrose passed him, Hazel managed to speak to her. 'Listen,' he whispered. 'I'll get you out sometime, somehow. Believe me.'

Primrose touched his

forepaw with hers. 'I do believe you, Hazel,' she said. She followed the other rabbits into the warren, turning back once to look at him, her eyes shining out of the darkness. Then she was gone.

Fiver spoke on, telling of the warren where Woundwort was born, of the Men who destroyed it, of Laurel dragging her young son to safety. Woundwort swayed on his feet as Fiver wailed, 'A weasel – coming closer – Laurel too tired to run –'

The memory of the moment when his mother was killed swept over Woundwort. He opened his mouth and the sound that came out was the cry of a young and desperate rabbit.

Fiver slumped, his vision over.

'Who *are* you?' said Woundwort, his eyes blank and empty.

Hazel seized his chance. 'Leaders of a great warren,' he said. 'You've seen what my brother can do. Let us go, or he'll haunt you forever.' Slowly he moved away, half-carrying the exhausted Fiver, heading for the ridge where Bigwig and Kehaar waited.

Woundwort stood silently, his head bowed.

'What are your orders, sir?' said Campion, after a while.

Slowly Woundwort raised his head. His eyes were full of hatred. 'Track them down,' he said. 'Find their warren and destroy it. No one gets the better of Woundwort. No one.'

Hazel, Bigwig and Fiver ran as fast as they could, but Campion and Vervain were strong rabbits and Woundwort was powered by rage. It seemed they were certain to be caught.

'This way,' called Kehaar, guiding them to the scarecrow field.

The straw man only fooled the Efrafans for a few moments, but it gave Hazel, Bigwig and Fiver the

chance to reach the railway ahead
of them. As they scrambled up the
embankment, the track began to
shake violently. With an extra burst
of speed they flung themselves
across. Woundwort and his captains
skidded to a halt on the wrong side
of the speeding train.

By the time the line of carriages
had passed, the Watership Down
rabbits were out of sight.

As they ran on they heard Woundwort's voice, growing fainter in the distance – 'I'll hunt you down. I'll get you. The world isn't big enough to hide you.'

Much later, when they dared to rest, Hazel said, 'What happened back there, Fiver? That was the strangest vision I've ever known you to have.'

'It nearly swept me away,' said Fiver. 'Woundwort is full of hate, and

44

fear, and loss. It was horrible.'

'It saved our lives,' said Hazel. He looked back the way they had come, his eyes full of sadness and longing. 'But Primrose is still in Efrafa.'

'And we've made an enemy who won't rest till Watership Down is destroyed,' said Fiver.

'This outing wasn't exactly a success, was it?' said Bigwig.

'No,' said Hazel. 'But don't worry. We'll be back.'

CHAPTER FOUR

Meeting the Hutch Rabbits

Hazel crept out of his burrow at dawn. He sniffed the air, scratched, and sat looking across the downs.

Hannah the fieldmouse looked up at him from under a dandelion clock. 'What's the matter, Hazel?' she said.

'Nothing,' said Hazel. 'I'm thinking.'

'You're not thinking,' said Hannah. 'You're worrying. It's different.'

Hazel sighed. 'You're right,' he said. 'And going to Efrafa didn't help.'

'That place!' said Hannah. 'It makes me shiver just hearing the stories.'

'Efrafa isn't all bad,' said Hazel.

'Aha,' said Hannah. 'Primrose.'

'Yes,' said Hazel. 'I want Primrose here. But we need lots more rabbits, too.'

Hannah pointed to the farm at the foot of the down. 'Try down there,' she said.

'Really?'

'Sure. It has hutch-rabbits!'

'Good idea!' said Hazel. He hurried into the warren to wake

Fiver and Pipkin.

'The farm?' said Fiver. 'But there's a cat.'

'And a big dog,' said Pipkin.

'Come on,' said Hazel. 'I can't rescue the hutch-rabbits on my own.'

Kehaar flew
with them part of
the way. 'Hazel need
nice girl-rabbit,' he said.

'The warren needs rabbits,' said
Hazel.

'Kehaar know about love,' said
the gull. 'He have gull-friend –
Natasha. But she go away.'

He gave a loud sob.

'Kehaar,' said Hazel firmly, 'go back and tell the others where we've gone.'

Kehaar flapped sadly away and the three rabbits made their way down to the edge of the farmyard.

They peeped out from behind an old mossy wall. The dog was tied to his kennel, sound asleep. There was no sign of the cat.

Hazel wanted to go in at once, but Fiver began to shudder, in the grip of a vision. 'Run fast, run hard,' he murmured. 'The Black Rabbit races across the yard.' He opened his eyes again. 'Oh, Hazel,' he said. 'The Black Rabbit of Inle is very close.'

'He's always close,' said Hazel briskly. 'Come on, we have work to do.'

They crossed the yard to the barn without disturbing the dog. Peering round the open barn door they saw a large rabbit hutch, on top of a pile of hay bales. Hazel left a nervous Pipkin on guard, and he and Fiver went inside.

'I don't like this,'
said Fiver.

'Let's just get on
with it,' said Hazel.

'It'll be nice to get
the old Hazel back,'
said Fiver, wistfully.

'What do you
mean?' said Hazel.

'You've been
dreaming about
Primrose since you
went to Efrafa,'
said Fiver. 'Now
you're charging
around like Bigwig
with a sore toe.'

'The old Hazel wasn't
clever enough to rescue
Primrose,' said
Hazel. 'Maybe
the new one
will do better.'
He climbed
the hay bales.
The hutch-
rabbits were
lying in a lazy
heap. They sat
up and looked
at him, but
only one of
them spoke.

'Hello,' she said. 'I'm Clover.
Where's your cage?'

'I haven't got a cage,' said Hazel.
'I live outside.'

The hutch-rabbits looked shocked
and Clover said, 'So who looks
after you?'

'We look after each other,' said Hazel. He began to chew through the leather door-hinge. 'I've come to help you escape,' he mumbled, his mouth full.

'Escape?' said Clover, surprised. 'All right, I'll give it a try.'

When the door fell off she hopped out, but the other hutch-rabbits weren't interested. They turned their backs and began to eat from their bowls.

'Cat!' squeaked Pipkin suddenly.

'Quick, Hazel!' yelled Fiver.

Hazel and Clover slid down the hay bales, but the cat was already slinking towards them, ears flat, tail lashing.

Hazel turned to face her. 'Fiver, Pipkin,' he shouted. 'Take Clover and run. I'll meet you in the lane.'

He dodged and darted in front of the angry cat, leading her on a wild dance around the barn.

The others raced outside, heading for the mossy wall. As they passed the kennel, the dog woke.

When Hazel guessed they were safe, he gave the cat the slip and dashed across the farmyard and out into the lane.

This time, the dog scrambled to his feet, barking furiously.

The farmhouse door opened and a Man stepped out. He raised a shotgun to his shoulder, took aim and fired.

Hazel leapt in the air – spun – and fell.

CHAPTER FIVE

Hazel and the Fire-stick

Behind the wall, Fiver, Pipkin and Clover crouched close to the ground as the sound of the shot echoed around them.

'What was that?' said Pipkin.

'A fire-stick,' said Clover. 'A Man-thing that lets him kill from far away.'

Fiver's ears drooped. 'I warned

Hazel,' he said. 'I told him the Black Rabbit was near.'

'Has the man got Hazel?' said Pipkin, close to tears.

Fiver closed his eyes and concentrated hard. Then he opened them again. 'Not yet,' he said. 'But we have to do something fast. Pipkin, do you know the way home?'

Pipkin looked towards the
distant hill of Watership Down,
with the beech tree on its crown.
'Yes,' he said.

'Then take Clover with you
and go,' said Fiver.
'I'll find Hazel.'

'How?'
said Pipkin.
'I don't know,'
said Fiver. 'I just will.'
He watched them
leave, then crept into the
lane. A shadow swept over him
and a harsh voice said, 'Hide!'
As Fiver ducked, Kehaar landed
beside him. 'Man in lane,' said the
gull. 'He have barking-stick.'

Kehaar listened as Fiver told him what had happened. Then he said, 'Barking-stick make big sound and throw black pebbles. If pebbles bite Hazel, he need help. You got special way of seeing, Fiver. Look for him.'

'My visions don't work like that,' said Fiver.

'Make 'em work,' said Kehaar.

Fiver squeezed his eyes shut and tried as hard as he could. Then his eyes opened wide. 'I heard Hazel calling,' he said. 'He's near. He sounded like he was inside something.'

'OK,' said Kehaar. 'Man gone. So now we look at inside places.'

They found a
hollow log, an
old bucket, an
abandoned burrow
– but no Hazel.

Then Fiver noticed a drainage pipe

 sticking out of
the hedge. 'He's
in there,' he said.
'I'm certain.'

'Alive in there?'
said Kehaar, 'Or dead in there?'

'I don't know,' said Fiver.

He called into the
pipe. There was
silence. Then a weak
voice said, 'Fiver, I
knew you'd find me.'

'I heard you calling,' said Fiver.

'I didn't call,' said Hazel, as Fiver and Kehaar climbed into the pipe.

'Then your spirit did,' said Fiver.

Kehaar began to peck carefully at the wound in Hazel's leg. Hazel squealed as the gull's sharp beak picked out the shotgun pellet and spat it away.

'Better now,' said Kehaar.

After a rest, Hazel was able to limp slowly home, with Fiver beside him and Kehaar gliding above.

The other rabbits hurried to greet them.

'You're safe!' said Pipkin.

'An adventure like
that,' said Bigwig, 'and you
left us behind!'

'You could have used some good
fighters,' said Hawkbit.

'Sometimes it's better to run,' said
Hazel. 'Clover, I'm glad you got out.
Sorry about the others.'

'Don't be,' said Clover. 'They're
happy where they are.'

Blackberry had put fresh bedding in Hazel's burrow and Fiver led his brother towards the warren entrance. 'Come inside and sleep,' he said.

Hazel turned back to look at the sunset, his face sad.

'Thinking about Primrose?' said Fiver.

'I promised I'd go back for her,' said Hazel.

'You will,' said Fiver. 'When you're strong again. You will.'

Glossary

Buck   A male rabbit

Doe   A female rabbit

Efrafa   The name of General
              Woundwort's warren

El-Arah   The shortened name of the
              rabbit hero, El-ahrairah. The
              many stories of El-Arah are
              an inspiration to all rabbits

Elil   Enemies of rabbits; like foxes,
              hawks and weasels

Flayrah   Good food; like carrots,
              cabbages and lettuces

Frith   The sun; a god to the rabbits

Frithmas   The rabbits' Christmas celebration; it is celebrated with a great feast

Inle   The moon; when it is time for a rabbit to die, the Black Rabbit of Inle comes to fetch him

Owsla   A group of strong brave rabbits who are trained to defend the warren

Silflay   Eating outside the warren; usually at dawn or dusk

Warren   The network of burrows where rabbits live

WATERSHIP™ DOWN

Join Hazel, Fiver, Bigwig and all their friends in these exciting new tales of friendship and bravery.

Escape to the Hills

Fiver's vision of the destruction of their warren has forced the rabbits to look for a new home. But can they survive the dangers of a long and hazardous journey?

ISBN: 0 09 940355 2
£2.99

WATERSHIP™ DOWN

Join Hazel, Fiver, Bigwig and all their friends in these exciting new tales of friendship and bravery.

Rabbits in Danger

Holly tells the Watership Down rabbits about a fine big warren where life is easy. But when they arrive, Fiver senses there's something that's not quite right...

ISBN: 0 09 940365 X
£2.99

WATERSHIP™ DOWN

Join Hazel, Fiver, Bigwig and all their friends in these exciting new tales of friendship and bravery.

Challenge to Efrafa

The Watership Down rabbits decide to help the unhappy rabbits at Efrafa to escape. But to do this they need to outwit the evil General Woundwort...

ISBN: 0 09 940335 8
£2.99

WATERSHIP™ DOWN

Join Hazel, Fiver, Bigwig and all their friends in these exciting new tales of friendship and bravery.

COMING SOON

The Hidden World

When Hazel, Hawkbit and Fiver fall down a hole in their warren, they find themselves buried in an underground tunnel. But where does it lead and can they find a way out?

AVAILABLE MARCH 2000

WATERSHIP™ DOWN

Join Hazel, Fiver, Bigwig and all their friends in these exciting new tales of friendship and bravery.

COMING SOON

Friend and Foe

The threat from Efrafa is growing all the time. So when Hazel finds the captain of their Owsla wounded, he tries to make friends with him and bring him round to their way of thinking.

AVAILABLE MARCH 2000